Mr. Murry and Thumbkin

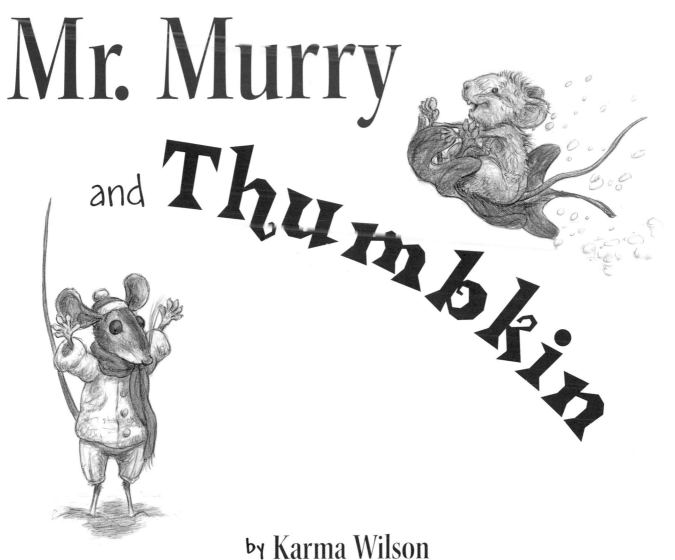

by Karma Wilson

Illustrated by Ard Hoyt

LITTLE, BROWN AND COMPANY

New York ∾ Boston

To my son Michael,
who has a room like Thumbkin's pumpkin and a heart like Mr. Murry's
—K.W

To my jewel, Emma,
beautiful and creative
—A.H.

Text copyright © 2004 by Karma Wilson
Illustrations copyright © 2004 by Ard Hoyt

Little, Brown and Company • Time Warner Book Group
1271 Avenue of the Americas, New York, NY 10020
Visit our Web site at www.lb-kids.com

First Edition

Library of Congress Cataloging-in-Publication Data

Wilson, Karma.
  Mr. Murry and Thumbkin / by Karma Wilson; illustrated by Ard Hoyt. — 1st ed.
    p. cm.
  Summary: While Mr. Murry Mouse worries too much, his neighbor Thumbkin is carefree, but with friendship their attitudes meet in the middle.
  ISBN 0-316-07613-9
  [1. Mice — Fiction. 2. Friendship — Fiction. 3. Stories in rhyme.] I. Title: Mr. Murry and Thumbkin. II. Hoyt, Ard, ill. III. Title.

PZ8.3.W6976Mr2004
[E] — dc21

2003054502

10 9 8 7 6 5 4 3 2 1

Book design by Saho Fujii

TWP

Printed in Singapore

The illustrations for this book were done in Prismacolor pencils on Canson paper.
The text was set in Veljovic Medium, and the display type is Kepler MM and Buckethead.

Once there was a furry mouse,
a skitter, scatter, scurry mouse,
a flurry-about-in-a-hurry mouse,
whose name was Mr. Murry Mouse.

He lived alone in an old teapot,
and Mr. Murry worried a LOT.

"Are the days too short?
Are the nights too cold?
Is my tail too long?
Are my teeth too old?"
He worried away each and every day.
Then . . .

Next door there moved another mouse
into a pretty pumpkin house,
a carefree country-bumpkin mouse
who went by the name of Thumbkin Mouse.

Thumbkin lay around all day
just gnawing on a stalk of hay.

He sang:
"Diddle-dee
and a fiddle-dee ho!
I got no worries,
oh, no no!"
And so . . .

He frittered away each and every day.

Now, Mr. Murry worried some more
about that new mouse living next door.
"His home is a shambles. The structure is poor.
Why, I've never seen such confusion before!"

Then, Mr. Murry, the neighborly sort,
took over a tasty raspberry torte.

"My name's Mr. Murry,
I've brought you a treat."

"Howdy, I'm Thumbkin.
Come in. Take a seat."

So, the two neighbors sat for a mouse-to-mouse chat.

Mr. Murry said, "Thumbkin, have you ever thought
this old pumpkin house is certain to rot?"

Thumbkin just chuckled. "Oh no, surely not.
Ya know, Mr. Murry, you worry a lot."

Mr. Murry said, "No, I'm a practical mouse,
and a pumpkin is quite an impractical house!

"And now I should go.
My chores will not keep.
I've windows to caulk
and a chimney to sweep."

Then he muttered, "Good day," and set off on his way.

The next afternoon, Mr. Murry stepped out.
"I've much that needs doing, of that there's no doubt.
 I'll rake and I'll mulch and I'll scour the grout."
And then he saw Thumbkin just lounging about!

He lay in his yard and admired his weeds,
he munched and he crunched upon fat pumpkin seeds.

"Mr. Murry, sit down.
It's a fine autumn day."
Mr. Murry said, "Oh,
but there's snow on the way.

"A sensible mouse would move out of that house!"

Thumbkin just laughed. "You sure fret and such.
If I stubbed my toe, you'd offer a crutch.
So what if my rooftop is saggin' a touch?
Ya know, Mr. Murry, you worry too much.

"While you fuss and fume, I'm gonna bake.
I hanker to whip up a sweet pumpkin cake."

Mr. Murry looked troubled.
"I have to advise
that serving your house
for dessert is unwise!"

He grumbled as Thumbkin sliced into his pumpkin.

After three weeks, in blew the first snow.

Mr. Murry cried, "Thumbkin, your roof looks so . . . low."

"I just love," said Thumbkin, "a good storm, ya know.

Relax, Mr. Murry. You do worry so."

But Thumbkin's poor house continued to sag.
And still Mr. Murry continued to nag.

"Perhaps we could save it.
We'll shore up the side.
We'll shingle the roof.
DO SOMETHING!" he cried.

Then a CREAK . . .

and a CRASH!

And a deafening SMASH!

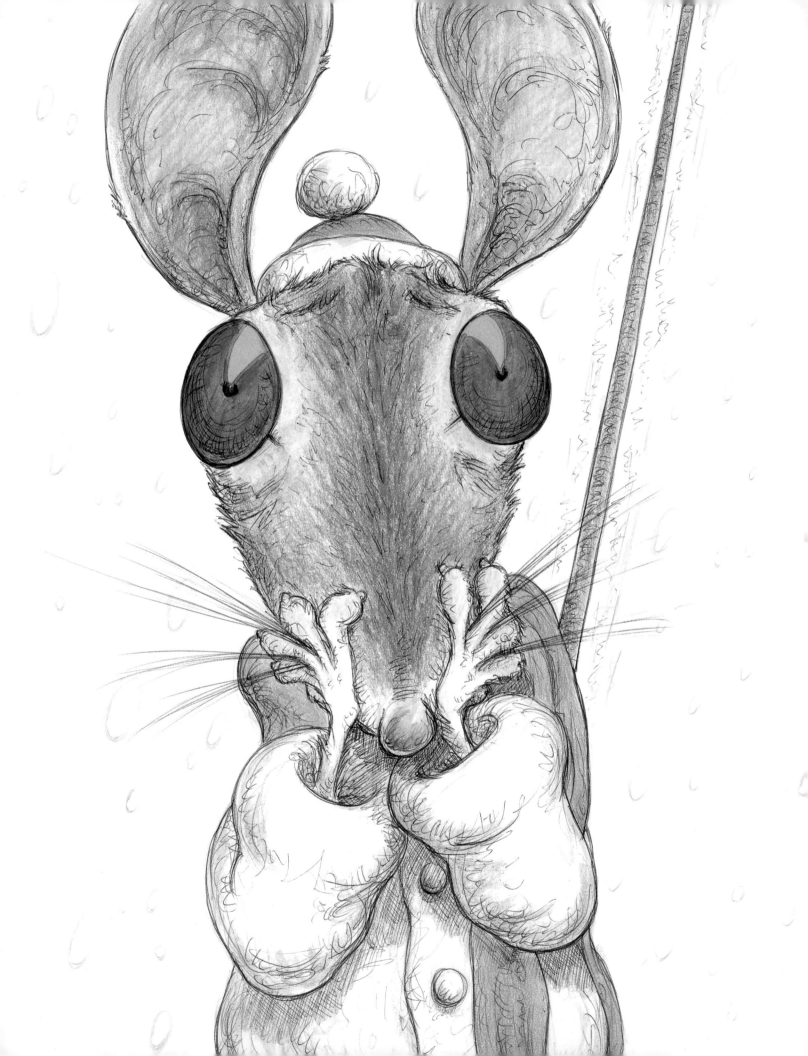

And all Mr. Murry's worries came true . . .
the two neighbors watched as that roof fell right through!
Mr. Murry cried, "Now what on earth shall you do?"
Thumbkin said, "Lie back and take in the view."

"I've always been keen on a breath of fresh air. The breeze is refreshin' and ruffles my hair.

"I got half a house,
I ain't needin' more."
Mr. Murry said, "Yes,
but what's left is all floor!"

"Aw, Mr. Murry," said Thumbkin,
"Don't worry."

That night, all alone, in his cozy teapot,
poor Mr. Murry, he worried a lot. . . .

He wrinkled his brow
and paced while he thought.
"Will Thumbkin freeze solid?
Oh, how could he not?

"Out in that snow, he'll chill through and through!

Hold on a minute, I know what I'll do. . . ."

So he bundled up warmly
and scurried next door.
"My teapot, dear Thumbkin,
has room for one more."

Thumbkin said, "R-r-really? It IS a mite ch-ch-illy."

And so the two friends settled in for the night.
They made up their beds, and they snuggled down tight.
Mr. Murry said, "Thumbkin, I'm worried, all right.
I've food for just one! What a horrible plight!"

"Aw, Mr. Murry," said Thumbkin. "Don't fear. . . .
We got half my pumpkin. We'll eat it all year!"

And so, Mr. Murry, who worried too much,
and Thumbkin, who worried too little . . .
lived out their days in a cozy teapot . . .
and met somewhere right in the middle.